The 12 Days of
CHRISTMAS

The 12 Days of
CHRISTMAS

Adapted by
Jane Cabrera

SCHOLASTIC INC.

ISBN 978-0-545-64302-3

12 11 10 9 8 7 6 5 4 3 2 1   13 14 15 16 17 18/0

Printed in the U.S.A.   40

First Scholastic printing, November 2013

The art was painted in acrylic paint, the same size as the book. The palettes were old china plates.
The artist started by tracing rough pencil drawings on paper taped onto a window.
The artist painted the black line, added the color, and finished with a little more black line.
The artist sometimes mixed the color on the actual artwork rather than on the palette.

The text typeface is Billy.

For Sonny

On the first day of Christmas,
my true love gave to me...

a party in a pear tree.

On the second day of Christmas,
my true love gave to me
2 drumming dogs

and a party in a pear tree.

On the third day of Christmas,
my true love gave to me
3 cute cats,

2 drumming dogs,
and a party in a pear tree.

On the fourth day of Christmas,
my true love gave to me
4 magic mice,

3 cute cats,
2 drumming dogs,
and a party
in a pear tree.

On the fifth day of Christmas,
my true love gave to me
5 shining stars,

4 magic mice,
3 cute cats,
2 drumming dogs,
and a party in a pear tree.

On the sixth day of Christmas,
my true love gave to me
6 bears a-snoozing,

5 shining stars,
4 magic mice,
3 cute cats,
2 drumming dogs,
and a party in a pear tree.

On the seventh day
of Christmas,
my true love gave to me
7 squirrels skiing,

6 bears a-snoozing,
5 shining stars,
4 magic mice,
3 cute cats,
2 drumming dogs,
and a party
in a pear tree.

On the eighth day of Christmas,
my true love gave to me
8 elves a-baking,

7 squirrels skiing,
6 bears a-snoozing,
5 shining stars,
4 magic mice,
3 cute cats,
2 drumming dogs,
and a party
in a pear tree.

On the ninth day of Christmas,
my true love gave to me
9 foxes sledding,

8 elves a-baking,
7 squirrels skiing,
6 bears a-snoozing,
5 shining stars,
4 magic mice,
3 cute cats,
2 drumming dogs,
and a party
in a pear tree.

On the tenth day of Christmas,
my true love gave to me
10 snowmen singing,

9 foxes sledding,
8 elves a-baking,
7 squirrels skiing,
6 bears a-snoozing,
5 shining stars,
4 magic mice,
3 cute cats,
2 drumming dogs,
and a party
in a pear tree.

On the eleventh day
of Christmas,
my true love gave to me
11 reindeer dancing,

10 snowmen singing,
9 foxes sledding,
8 elves a-baking,
7 squirrels skiing,
6 bears a-snoozing,
5 shining stars,
4 magic mice,
3 cute cats,
2 drumming dogs,
and a party
in a pear tree.

On the twelfth day of Christmas,
my true love gave to me
12 penguins skating,

11 reindeer dancing,
10 snowmen singing,
9 foxes sledding,
8 elves a-baking,
7 squirrels skiing,
6 bears a-snoozing,
5 shining stars,
4 magic mice,
3 cute cats,
2 drumming dogs,
and a . . .

sleigh ride home for me!

THE 12 DAYS OF CHRISTMAS

Original lyrics by Jane Cabrera

Traditional carol